WITHDRAWN

08-07

Gioconda Belli – Wolf Erlbruch

The Butterfly
Workshop

*Translated from the Spanish
by Charles Castaldi*

Europa
editions

Europa Editions
116 East 16th Street
12th floor
New York, N.Y. 10003
www.europaeditions.com
info@europaeditions.com

Translation by Charles Castaldi
Original Title: *El taller de las mariposas*

Belli, Gioconda / Erlbruch, Wolf
The Butterfly Workshop

Library of Congress Cataloging in Publication Data is available
ISBN 1-933372-12-5

First Publication 2006 by Europa Editions

Book design by Emanuele Ragnisco
www.mekkanografici.com

Printed in Italy
Arti Grafiche La Moderna – Rome

This tale is for Ana Maria
Who smiles every time
A butterfly beats its wings.
And for Lutz and Salva
Who always see her smile.

THE BUTTERFLY WORKSHOP

B utterflies are almost weightless. They are ever so light, like the batting of an eyelid, the sun blinking red and yellow.

They come in so many colors, you might think it's a rainbow sneezing—*atchoo*—all those little pieces fluttering down to earth.

But there was a time, long ago, when there were no butterflies. None.

In those days, the Designers of All Things could design animals for the Animal Kingdom and flowers, fruits and vegetables for the Plant Kingdom. But they had to follow one very strict rule: they were not allowed to mix animals and plants.

Among the designers, however, there was a restless boy named Odair who found this rule quite bothersome because he couldn't help thinking of different ways to mix the species. Odair was very handy and he was constantly assembling strange objects. He would meet with a group of friends in a Cave Hidden Deep in the Forest where they would talk about all the things that could be created if only the Designers of All Things were a bit more daring and less strict about their rules.

"A tree that could sing like a bird, or a bird that would lay fruit instead of eggs," Odair would explain to his friends.

Odair's secret obsession, however, was to combine a bird and a flower. This was his dream project, something he thought about day and night, even though he couldn't figure out what a creature that would fly like a bird and have the beauty of a flower would actually look like.

Odair and his friends spent a great deal of time in the Cave Hidden Deep in the Forest coming up with new inventions. This worried the Ancient Wise Woman, who was in charge of the Designers of All Things, so she decided she needed to do something to prevent Odair's ideas from spreading and upsetting the harmony of creation.

So the Ancient Wise Woman summoned Odair and his friends and reprimanded them severely.

"The order of the cosmos is based on harmony, on rules that are perfect in their simplicity. So that you may learn that even the smallest things are designed with wisdom and that the laws of creation should not be taken lightly, we have decided to transfer you to a new job," she announced.

And with that the Ancient Wise Woman pulled back a heavy curtain to reveal a dusty old workshop whose walls were covered with spiderwebs.

"From now on you will work in the Insect Workshop," she told them.

The Insect Workshop had a pretty bad reputation among the Designers of All Things. They looked down on it because insects were tiny and their main job was carrying things or cleaning the forest of dry leaves and rotten wood. Also, they often stung the larger animals and their larvae ate the leaves of trees. The Designers of Insects were very shy. They wore thick glasses and kept to themselves. Their great achievement was to have made the spiders, whose strong and perfectly woven webs made them very proud.

"But insects are not beautiful," Odair protested.

"Who says they can't be?" argued the Ancient Wise Woman. "You can make them beautiful. It's up to you. You have the freedom to design them as you wish. You can design many different kinds of insects: insects that sing or look like plants, that resemble grasses and leaves. The only rule you must respect is not to mix the Plant Kingdom with the Animal Kingdom."

Odair and his friends left the Ancient Wise Woman's house feeling quite downcast. That night, after dinner, they met in the Cave Hidden Deep in the Forest to talk about their bad luck.

"Look where we've ended up: insect design!" said Logan tapping nervously on a rock.

Everyone was silent until Aretta exclaimed: "We could design an insect that twinkles like a star and call it Firefly!"

"We could design an insect that sings louder than a bird and call it Cricket!" said May.

"We could design one that jumps like a kangaroo and call it Grasshopper!" said John.

Little by little their bad moods were forgotten as they all pitched in ideas for the many types of insects they could design.

"I will design an insect that will look like a tiny turtle except that its shell will be red with black dots . . . It will be a Ladybug," cried Billy.

"And I will design one that rolls into a ball when anyone touches it, a Rolly-Polly," said Odair.

Eventually they went to sleep excited that their new job would, after all, give them many opportunities to create many beautiful and fun designs.

Odair busied himself for several days in the Insect Workshop designing complex iridescent creatures. He also created a tiny but very strong insect he named Ant. But he still wasn't satisfied. His obsession with making a creature that would combine the beauty of a bird and a flower came back to haunt him. He didn't like being in the Insect Workshop with its cobweb walls and its ancient, bespectacled designers. He preferred to go and sit by the pond and lose himself in his thoughts.

In the world of the Designers of All Things there were regions where the seasons never changed. For example, it was always winter where the designers of large cold-climate animals lived so that they could give plenty of thought to the design of the great Polar Bears and of the Penguin's elegant suits.

It was always summer on the banks of the pond where Odair liked to sit. The sun was always shining high in the sky, the trees were green and heavy with fruit and countless species of birds sang and flew pirouettes in the breeze. Mesmerized, Odair would look at the colorful beauty of Nature, asking himself over and over how to make his dream come true, how to make something that would be both bird and flower; a creature that would dazzle every time it opened its wings.

His transfer to the Insect Workshop and the Ancient Wise Woman's prohibition had made his task even more difficult. Odair really didn't like insects. Aretta tried to convince him that insects were important, that they were messengers for trees and flowers that couldn't move around like animals did. She was very proud to have made the Bee which took pollen from flower to flower and also produced delicious honey. But Odair thought that the Bee was hairy, fat and noisy. What he wanted to design would be breathtakingly beautiful. It would be sublime, like the rainbow his grandfather had designed after he dreamt that the Sun was splashing in the water.

Odair's friends tried to console him, but the boy was turning quieter and more solitary with each passing day. At night, while everybody else was resting, Odair would be hunched over his drafting table in the workshop, doing one drawing after the other, trying combination after combination and yet never coming up with exactly what he wanted.

Soon, the more experienced designers were laughing at Odair's experiments.

"Look at that stubborn boy," they would remark, "as if it were possible to design something that surpasses what already exists."

One night Odair ran out of the workshop screaming. He had attached wings made out of a fine membrane to a cute little mouse he had seen running around the room and he had ended up with a small, black, rather ugly animal: the Bat. While he was running away from his own creation, Odair could hear the laughter of the others making fun of him.

"You must be careful, Odair." The Ancient Wise Woman admonished him. "By trying to design something perfect you might end up creating monsters. Your obsession with making life more pleasant and beautiful might, if you're not careful, result in pain and fear for the other creatures that inhabit Nature."

"But I just want to make something awesome," sobbed Odair.

"There are many pitfalls on the road to beauty and perfection. Many have lost the way. You must be careful," repeated the Ancient Wise Woman.

The next day, when Odair went to sit at his usual place by the pond he found a dog resting there.

"This is my spot," Odair said. "Please let me sit down."

"Okay, I'll move over," answered the Dog. "I can get comfortable anywhere. Just having a place to lie down makes me happy."

"Ah!" Odair sighed. "Sometimes I wish I could be like you, happy just letting things be the way they are, but I can't. I can't rest

until I design something that is as beautiful as the combination of a bird and a flower."

"Why make your life so difficult?" the Dog said. "No one cares that the thing you want to design doesn't exist. Take it easy, live your life, don't bother anybody and nobody will bother you."

"But I have a dream that can bring more beauty and harmony to the world," said Odair. "If I give it up just because others don't

understand and make fun of me, I would have to stop believing in beauty and in the importance of pursuing one's dreams until the end."

"I don't dream of doing anything," the Dog yawned. "I am content just lying in the grass, eating, sleeping and going for walks with anyone who'll take me."

"Your life is very simple because you've never felt responsible for anything," Odair said.

"If someone tries to harm my owner, I defend him. I feel responsible for that," the Dog replied.

"I see," said Odair. "But for me there's more to life than just feeling safe. I feel a responsibility to make life more pleasant for others. I'd like to think that many plants, animals and humans would appreciate the beauty of my designs . . . if I'm able to achieve my goal one day."

"You'll get there," said the Dog, standing up on all fours, looking a bit bored with the conversation and giving himself a good stretch.

"How do you know?" Odair asked.

"Because that's what happens to me. If I dream of a bone when I'm sleeping and I keep dreaming about it after waking, there's a very good chance I'll find it."

And with that the Dog took off, bounding happily through the grass.

O dair sat for a long time thinking about what the Dog had said, and then he returned to the Insect Workshop to experiment with newer and newer designs.

Late that night, after having worked many hours, Odair thought he might have actually achieved his dream. He had made a long, resplendent insect with a double set of rapidly beating transparent wings which gave off a silver glint. He blew on the drawing to give the new design flight and two dragonflies hovered around the room. He gently caught one of them with his fingers and went to look for his friend Aretta.

Odair and Aretta contemplated the Dragonfly gliding through the moonlight.

"It's magnificent," Aretta said. "It's as fast as a hummingbird."

"It's quite exquisite," Odair said thoughtfully, "but what I'm dreaming of is even more beautiful."

"What's wrong with you, Odair? The World is so full of beauty. You must learn to be humble and realize that often things cannot be the way we want them to be."

"But, Aretta, we are the Designers of All Things. If we gave up our dreams what sense would our lives make?"

"Maybe you've set yourself too difficult a goal," she said.

"Exactly why I have to keep trying," said Odair with determination.

And Odair continued his experiments in the Insect Workshop in spite of the laughter of the others, in spite of the sad looks his friends gave him; in spite of the fact many openly said he was just being stubborn. Odair's existence became quite solitary. He wandered the forests and mountains alone.

"Beautiful things are delicate," the Wind told him. "Look how I strip the bushes of their flowers by simply puffing my cheeks and blowing."

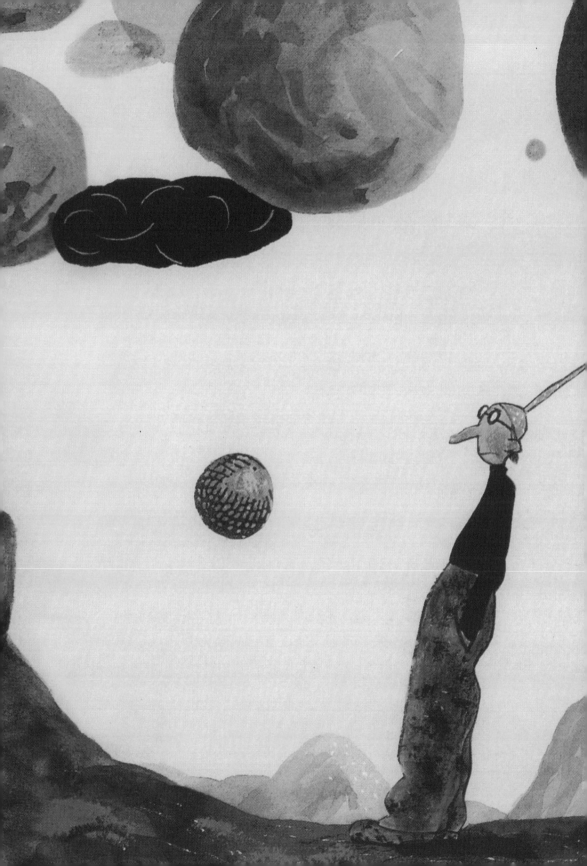

"And look at me," said the Volcano. "Just one sneeze and my ashes destroy whatever they touch."

"But flowers grow back and the grass sprouts anew," Odair said. "That's what I like about Beauty, it never gives up."

"But what good is a flower? What is its purpose?" a black Rock asked. "It withers and dies so quickly."

"It becomes fruit," Odair said. "And it's beautiful. Beauty can't be explained, it must be felt."

"Beauty is like when I race through the sky illuminating everything I touch," said the Lightning Bolt.

"But you're scary," said the snake.

"Look who's talking," responded the Lightning Bolt.

"I want to design something that brings joy to people," Odair said as he walked off along the bank of a stream.

One day, Odair had a dream. He dreamt that his grandfather had been blowing very hard on a Rainbow and the Rainbow had broken into little pieces that had taken wing. Odair woke with a start and tried to draw the tiny Rainbow fragments, but he only managed to draw a cicada that took off from the page, singing.

Late that afternoon, thinking of his grandfather, tears of frustration welling in his eyes, he fell asleep at the edge of the pond.

He was awakened by the buzzing of wings grazing his ear. He sat up, rubbed his eyes and just then saw a Hummingbird dipping its long beak into the center of a blue flower. The Hummingbird flew from flower to flower, drinking nectar from all the blooms along the shore where Odair sat. Then the tiny creature dashed off across the water toward a rose bush on the far shore.

Odair stared at it, mesmerized. Then, thinking he might never design anything so beautiful, he lowered his gaze sadly. And that's when he noticed the Hummingbird's shadow hovering on the pond's surface which glistened with the blues and pinks of the set-

ting sun. The tiny shadow seemed to have a life of its own. It moved, it flickered, it changed; one moment it was a bird, the next, a flower. Odair's heart leaped. Yes! There it was. Finally! The combination he had been looking for all this time; the perfect mix of flower and bird. He was seeing it right there on the pond's surface! He had found his design. And he would call it, Butterfly.

He raced back to the workshop and began to feverishly draw the wings and the body of the Butterfly. To make the wings as light and graceful as possible, he made them of tiny overlapping scales, like the tiles on the roof of a house. Then he drew a slim insect's body and gave it a very long tongue to

plunge into the flowers for honey, and hairy little feet so that pollen could travel from one flower to the next.

When he had finished his drawing, he called his friends Aretta, Billy, May and Logan and took them to the Cave Hidden Deep in the Forest to show them his design. After lighting dozens of candles, he blew on the drawing, and to the amazement of his wide-eyed friends, a deep orange butterfly with yellow stripes across its wings flew off the paper.

"It's a flying flower," May gasped.

"It's a small bird," cried Billy at the same time.

"You did it!" Aretta exclaimed.

"And to think we doubted you," Billy said, somewhat ashamed.

"Never again will we laugh at other people's dreams."
They all hugged and, shedding tears of joy, they embraced Odair.
"We haven't broken the rules of creation," Odair said cheerfully once they dried their tears and quieted down. "The Butterfly will be an insect but it will be as beautiful as a flower and fast as a bird.

Humans will admire its beauty and they will put it in their stories and myths. Each pair of wings will be dazzling. If you all agree, we'll ask to have our own workshop, a workshop dedicated to designing Butterflies.

They looked at Odair, unable to contain their excitement. That

a Designer would ask to have an exclusive workshop was quite an extraordinary event. The Ancient Wise Woman had to call a special council to be attended by all Designers and their craftspeople. The new creation would be presented at the gathering and if everyone applauded and approved they would be given their very own Workshop.

"We would have to design hundreds of Butterflies for the presentation," said May.

"I have everything figured out," Odair announced. "We'll work in secret and surprise everybody."

The following day everyone arrived very early at the Insect Workshop and met at Odair's drafting table.

"First of all," Odair said, "we'll have to distract the others."

As he talked he was busily drawing a multitude of small, black, fast flying insects.

"We'll make this bothersome insect that will never know when to stop pestering people. We'll call it Fly."

As he said this, Odair cracked open the door to the main drafting room and blew softly over the paper where he had drawn hundreds of flies. The flies took off and began landing on inkbottles, eyeglasses, paint jars, hair, clothes and ears of the poor Insect Designers.

The old Designers got so involved in stopping the flies from bothering them, that they didn't have the time or energy to worry about what the young Designers were doing at Odair's drafting table.

For many days Odair and his friends worked behind closed doors, listening to the music of a creature who, after his birth, would be called Beethoven. Inspired by the music, they imagined all the varied and lovely places on Earth that would be inhabited by Butterflies. They designed Butterflies for tropical jungles, for temperate forests, for prairies and steppes.

At the end of the fifth day, Odair paid a visit to the Ancient Wise

Woman and asked her to convene a special council to present his new creation.

The Ancient Wise Woman was surprised because she hadn't heard anything about a new creature. She asked Odair repeatedly if he was sure it was an insect, if he was certain he had not broken any of the laws of creation.

"It is an insect," Odair insisted.

"Are you sure your creature is worthy of a meeting of the special council? Are you sure that you won't disappoint us?" she insisted.

"I am certain," Odair answered.

Impressed by his determination, the Ancient One didn't have the heart to deny him his wish after all the effort and suffering he had endured. She accepted his request and called a special council for the next day.

The Council Hall was magnificent and only used for special occasions. It had a crystal ceiling and the walls were made of the same material as the clouds. It was located in a region of eternal spring, so the light inside was always that of a sunny day in early May.

Odair and his friends had worked all night without stopping and they were quite exhausted when they arrived at the council carrying enormous crystal containers whose contents were hidden by cloths.

Having been summoned by the Ancient Wise Woman, the Designers of All Things began to arrive.

The Designers of Large Animals came first. They were red-headed giants and they had designed the Lion, the Elephant, the Giraffe and the Rhinoceros.

Then came the Designers of Cats. They had almond-shaped eyes and they moved silently and sinuously.

The Designers of Dogs were young and boisterous. They had grown tails from designing so many dogs and they were wagging them excitedly now.

The Designers of Sea Life were thin and had translucent skin. They wore hats made of fish scales that glittered in the sunlight.

Moving imperceptibly, the silent Designers of Trees arrived dressed in rich green fabrics. They were accompanied by the short and chubby Designers of Bushes and the Designers of Flowers, who were breathtakingly beautiful with their fair faces so colorfully made up and their dresses of woven petals.

The Designers of Birds flew in wrapped in resplendent feather capes. They kept their distance from the Designers of Reptiles, who were quite somber and had bodies so supple they could slide through the thinnest of cracks.

Finally, the thundering, stony footfalls of the Designers of Metals announced their arrival. They were trailed by the luminous and almost invisible Designers of Planets and Stars.

Everybody had assembled. The doors were about to close when, tentatively, the bespectacled Designers of Insects arrived, their arms still twitching from having shooed away so many flies.

Odair and his friends were very nervous. Aretta's hands were sweaty and Billy, not knowing what to do with his, kept putting them in and out of his pockets.

The murmur of countless conversations filled the Council Hall. Everyone was wondering what the kids could have designed to deserve such a meeting. Those who had laughed at Odair were upset at having had to interrupt their work for this stubborn boy. They figured it was impossible he could have designed anything that merited his own workshop.

At last, the Ancient Wise Woman took her place at the head of the Council Hall and the room went silent.

Odair asked for all the windows to be closed. The kids stood by each of the crystal boxes at the front of the Great Hall and at a signal from Odair they lifted the sheets and opened the crystal boxes one by one.

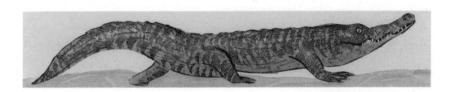

Myriads of multi-colored butterflies filled the air with reds, blues, yellows, violets, oranges, greens and whites. They flew in perfect rainbow formation over the heads of the stunned audience. Odair clapped and the butterflies broke out of formation and combined into waves of solid colors that drew gasps from the crowd. Another clap from Odair and the butterflies alighted on the highest part of the crystal ceiling to show off the underside of their wings which resembled tropical vegetation, temperate forests, prairies and snow-capped mountains.

The Ancient Wise Woman was moved to tears. It happened to her every time she experienced a thing of immense beauty. The boy had done it! The Butterfly was truly the perfect blend of flower and bird. No wonder! After all, Odair was the grandson of the Designer of the Rainbow. Following family tradition, he had designed a delicate creature whose beauty would leave an indelible impression in the hearts of plants, animals and humans.

The Designers of All Things also could not contain their astonishment. They couldn't take their eyes off these marvelous Butterflies, hovering about like weightless flowers, showing off the delicate architecture of their wings and the audacity of their design.

Those who had scoffed at Odair kept examining the butterflies resting on their hands, their downcast eyes hiding the embarrassment they felt for having doubted him.

Then, with a swish of their woven petal dresses, the Designers of Flowers stood and started clapping with their delicate hands. Soon the others followed and a rousing applause filled every corner of the Great Hall in honor of the new creation.

Odair could sense that everyone in the Great Hall was enjoying the vision of planet Earth populated by butterflies. He realized that his sleepless nights, his loneliness, sadness and anguish, had not been in vain. All those feelings and tears had also made the Butterfly.

S o that it would be clear that to make a thing of beauty takes hard work, he thought he would make the Butterfly begin as a caterpillar who then would transform into one of the most marvelous creatures of creation.

He realized that his friend, the Dog, had been right: dreams could come true. The secret was never to tire of dreaming. And never to give up.

Odair built his workshop on the edge of the Hummingbird Pond with walls made of pieces of rainbow. Since that day, he and his friends have designed hundreds of thousands of Butterflies.